This book is dedicated with love to all the angels
at Best Friends Animal Sanctuary in Kanab, Utah.

Library of Congress Cataloging-in-Publication Data
Spowart, Robin.
Inside, outside Christmas/by Robin Spowart.—1st ed. p. cm.
Summary: A mouse family engages in activities both inside and outside
that are associated with Christmas such as buying and hiding gifts.

ISBN 0-8234-1370-5 (reinforced)
[1. Christmas—Fiction. 2. Mice—Fiction. 3. Stories in rhyme.]
I. Title.
PZ8.3.S763In 1998   [E]—dc21   97-41956 CIP AC

Design: Yvette Lenhart

Inside, Outside
CHRISTMAS

Robin Spowart

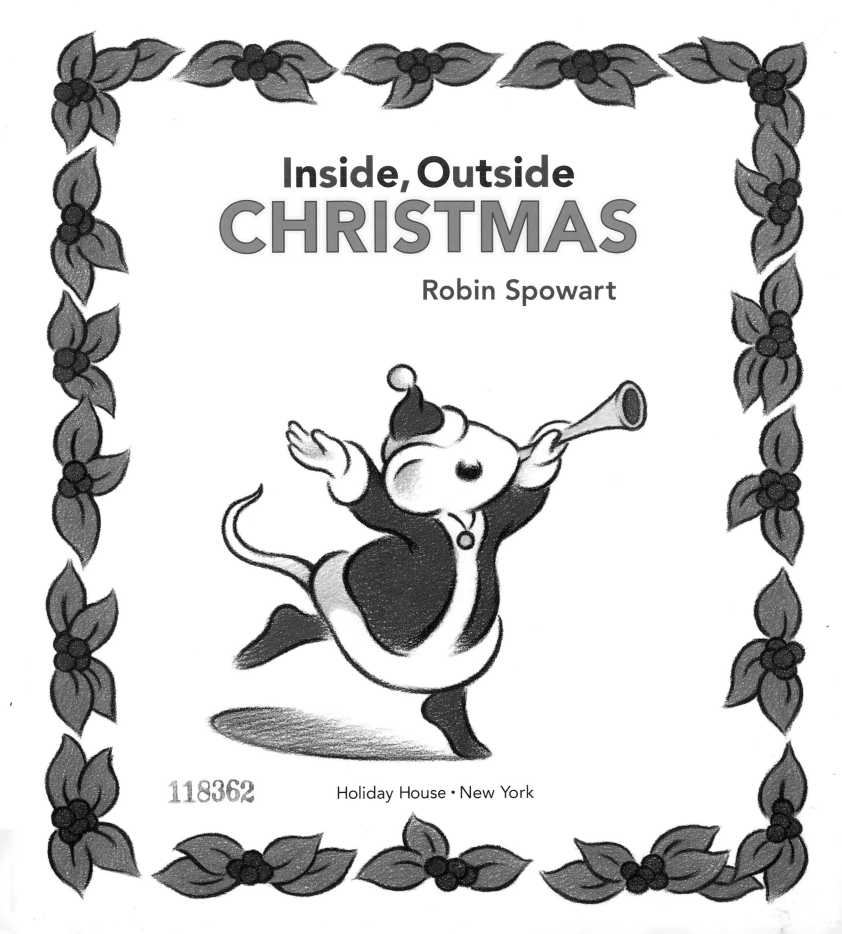

Holiday House • New York

Inside, stringing

Outside, bringing

Inside, cooking

Outside, looking

Inside, singing

Outside, ringing

Inside, munching

Outside, crunching

Inside, tying

Outside, buying

Inside, hiding

Outside, sliding

Inside, sharing

Outside, caring

Inside, writing

Outside, lighting

Inside, mingling

Outside, jingling

Inside, waiting

Outside, skating

Inside, love

Outside, love